This Book Belongs To:

_____

_____

Acknowledgements

I would like to thank the team at Team Author UK for all their help and assistance in creating this book. Special thanks to Sarah Parkinson for her beautiful illustrations.

I would also like to thank Alice Bennett for her patience and technological support.

The King And The Shell
Written by Rowena Swanson
Illustrated by Sarah Parkinson

First published in 2021
ISBN: 978-1-3999-0310-3
Raven Star Books

Children's Book Publishers
A Division of Team Author UK

The King and the Shell

Written by Rowena Swanson
Illustrated by Sarah Parkinson

I dedicate this book to my daughter Eva Ocean with fondest childhood memories

The old King sat in his favourite armchair, beside the fire, in his castle overlooking the sea.

His dogs sat patiently on the rug beside him. The King noticed the moon shining through the castle window.

He rose to look out over the sea. He noticed
a shimmering object at the water's edge;
it shone brightly in the moonlight,
sparkling like a diamond.

The King put on his boots
and majestic coat, and
with his dogs wandered
down the winding path
to the beach.

The King was sure he could hear music; as he got closer to the water's edge he could see that the object was a beautiful seashell. He picked it up and put it in his pocket and returned up the path to his castle.

The King put the shell on the mantelpiece above the fire. He sat beside the fire and fell asleep.

The King was woken at sunrise by the sound of strange music, and then a voice said, "Help me, please help me, it's hot up here!"

The King went over to the mantelpiece to investigate the strange voice.

The voice said, "Take me home. Take me back to the sea!"

The King picked up the shell.

"What is this, a talking shell?"

"Take me back to the sea, I am alive and will surely die up here," said the shell.

"But you are my ornament, I want to keep you. I am the King, this is my kingdom and I shall do as I please," said the King.

"Please! The ocean will die and so will I if you do not take me back to the sea. It is my home, where I belong," said the shell.

"Why should I? Finders, keepers," said the King.

"If you take me back to the sea, you will help save the ocean and I will show you the mermaids," said the shell.

"Mermaids!" said the King. "In that case, I will indeed take you back to the sea."

So, the King put the shell into his pocket and wandered back down the winding path to the sea.

He reluctantly placed the shell at the
water's edge and she swam into the ocean.

The King waited, but he was impatient. All was quiet, the sun was slowly rising, with just the sound of the waves crashing on the shore.

"Where are the mermaids? I have been tricked by a shell!" exclaimed the King.

Then all of a sudden, two mermaids appeared in the sea.
The King stood on the shore staring in amazement.

"Come into the sea and join us?" asked the mermaids.

"I cannot swim!" said the King. "Come closer." said the King.

"We cannot come onto the land. Will you build us a sandcastle?" the mermaids asked.

"Where is the shell? How will I see her again?" asked the King.

"You will hear her call when she sings. Then you will know that the ocean is alive and well. Just listen to the sound of the sea," said the mermaids.

With that, the mermaids disappeared into the ocean, waving to the King as they went. He waved back.

The King promised to protect the mermaids and all the sea life and shells in the ocean forever more.

What a story to tell his grandchildren!

I'm free!

About the Author

Rowena Swanson was born in Wallasey, Wirral. She now lives in Liverpool. Rowena has a Crafts Degree and a Postgraduate Diploma in Screenwriting. 'The King and the Shell' is her debut children's picture book. She hopes the book will inspire children to take care of nature and the environment.

The story was inspired by a gap year spent in Australia many moons ago.

It has taken 20 years to fulfil her dream and see this project come to fruition.

Many more stories in the archive yet to be realised.

f @RavenStarBooks   O @RavenStarBooks   🐦 @RavenStarBooks

About the Illustrator

Sarah Parkinson is an Amazon Bestselling Illustrator and Author of 'The Tales of Willow Park' children's book series. Whilst living in Shropshire with her husband and daughter, she discloses some illustrator secrets teaching children of all ages how to draw with her Art classes. Sarah publishes her books with the assistance of Team Author UK and enjoyed working with them so much that she became part of the team as an Illustrator in 2021.

For more information, go to Facebook:

f @Sparky Author - Sarah Parkinson

Printed in Great Britain
by Amazon